This book belongs to:

_____

_____

_____

Other books in the Big J series:

Big J and the Hockey Stick

COMING SOON

Big J and the Fire Station

Big J and the Great Outdoors

BIG J and the BIRTHDAY PARTY

Lynn Gale
Jenn Anderson

Big J has a best friend and his name is Charlie. He lives in the country on a farm.

Charlie's birthday is next week and he's having a party. Big J is so excited to visit his friend and see a real farm!

Big J shops with his mom for a gift. Charlie likes trucks, so Big J chooses a monster truck with huge wheels. He helps his mom wrap it and then prints Charlie's name on the tag.

Finally, it's the day of the party! Big J can't wait to see real cows, pigs, and horses!

His cousin Norah is excited because she gets to come to the party and play with Charlie's little sister, Mabel.

Big J is so surprised at how big the farm is!

Norah goes inside the house with Mabel. There are kittens to play with in there!

The party is in the barn. There are lights strung up, tables of gifts and food, and games to play.

It doesn't smell good in the barn. Big J crinkles his nose.

There's hay, too. It makes Big J sneeze and his eyes water. He feels like he wants to go home, but he doesn't say anything.

The farm isn't what he expected at all.

The party starts with a hayride and Charlie's dad helps the kids get on the wagon. Big J can't stop sneezing from the hay.

When they get back, they play in the barn.

There are kids at the party that Big J doesn't know and he feels a bit left out.

They invite him to shoot rubber arrows at hay bales, but he's too shy to join in.

It's time to ride the horses. Charlie's dad brings Big J's horse over and it looks huge! Big J isn't sure he wants to ride after all.

Charlie's dad explains how to get up and how to hold on, which makes Big J feel better.

They ride around the farm. Each horse follows the horse in front of them like a trail ride.

They get to the field where the cows graze. There are a lot of cows! Big J is afraid.

He forgets how to hold on to his saddle and when he lets go, he slides off onto the ground into the mud!

His butt and elbow hurt, but he's okay.

Charlie's dad lifts him up onto his horse and lets him sit in front. Big J likes riding together better than alone.

And he gets to be the leader of the trail ride!

When they get back to the barn, it's time to sing to Charlie before he opens his gifts. They have a contest to see who can sing Happy Birthday the loudest.

Big J tries to sing, but he can't stop sneezing from the hay. He claps along instead.

Next, Charlie opens his gifts. He loves the monster truck so much, he runs over and gives Big J a high five.

Big J is happy that Charlie likes his gift. This time when the kids invite him to play, he says yes.

Then it's time to go home. Big J's dad and mom are waiting outside the barn with Norah. Big J says goodbye and thank you to Charlie. He even remembers to wish him a happy birthday.

Charlie's mom gives Big J and Norah each a wrapped piece of cake. Norah hands her piece to her auntie to carry. They get into the van to go home.

"Did you two
like the farm?"
Big J's dad asks.

Big J thinks about the hayride, riding with Charlie's dad on the horse, the piece of birthday cake in his lap, and his new friends. "Yes!" he yells. Then he eats his cake.

Norah hollers "ME TOO!"then giggles. She has a surprise for her mom and dad. There is a kitten hidden in her jacket!

The kitten doesn't say anything, she just licks Norah's hand.

"When can we go back?" Big J asks.
"It was the best birthday party ever!"

Then he falls asleep with hay in his
hair and frosting on his cheeks.

The end.

ACTIVITIES

1. Can you find at least 12 baby chicks throughout the story?
2. Can you find the 3 ants in the pictures?
3. Can you find 3 mice in the pictures?
4. Can you find the sneaky fox that is hiding somewhere in the story?
5. When Norah leaves the farm, did you know what she had hiding in her jacket?

Dedicated to Jonah and Norah, with love.

First edition 2024

Edited and Formatted by Jess Schultz, Sweet Simple Collabs

ISBN 978-1-7390527-7-5 (ebook)
ISBN 978-1-7390527-8-2(paperback)
ISBN 978-1-7390527-6-8 (hardcover)

The illustrations in this book were done in watercolour
using Daniel Smith paints on Arches 100% cotton 140 lb. watercolour paper.
Some images were enhanced digitally.

Windsong Publishing Canada
Alberta, Canada
www.windsongpublishingcanada.com

Visit us at www.lynngalewriter.com and
https://www.instagram.com/creative_j0urney/.

Lynn Gale, Author

Lynn Gale is a poet, writer, and gramma. She lives and creates word stories in Alberta. Big J and the Birthday Party is Book 2 of Big J's adventures and she is already creating more stories in this series.

Jenn Anderson, Illustrator

Jenn Anderson is a creative heart who expresses her thoughts through colour and pictures. She loved every minute of illustrating this book and can't wait to see what Big J gets up to next.

Printed in the USA
CPSIA information can be obtained
at www.ICGtesting.com
LVHW062114170424
777693LV00002B/98